XF   Kroll, Virginia L.
KRO   Mosquito
                    FRA
2011

O9-BTJ-582

ST. MARY PARISH LIBRARY
FRANKLIN, LOUISIANA

MOSQUITO

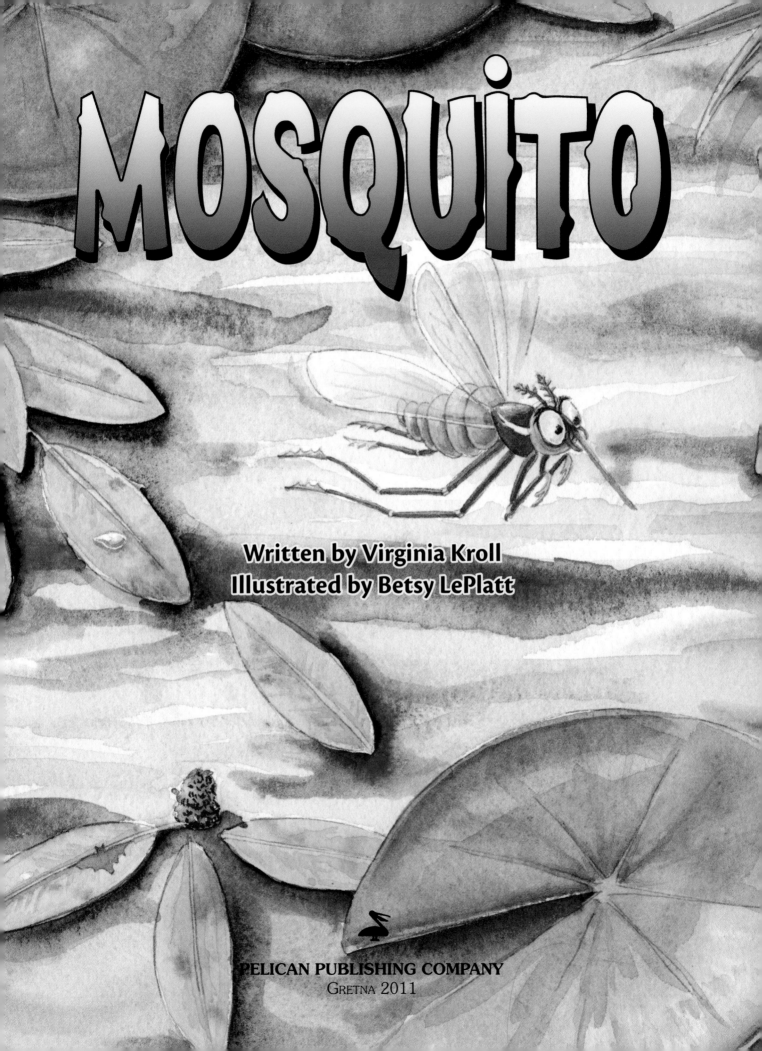

MOSQUITO

Written by Virginia Kroll
Illustrated by Betsy LePlatt

PELICAN PUBLISHING COMPANY
GRETNA 2011

With love to Reese Kinley and Dylan Russell—V. K.

Copyright © 2011
By Virginia Kroll

Illustrations copyright © 2011
By Betsy LePlatt
All rights reserved

---

*The word "Pelican" and the depiction of a pelican are
trademarks of Pelican Publishing Company, Inc., and are
registered in the U.S. Patent and Trademark Office.*

Library of Congress Cataloging-in-Publication Data

Kroll, Virginia L.
  Mosquito / by Virginia Kroll ; illustrated by Betsy LePlatt.
     p. cm.
  Summary: Mosquito buzzes around many different animals and
hears "Vamoose" from Moose, "Oh, nuts!" from Squirrel, and "Good
heavens!" from Girl, but the tables are turned when Bat arrives.
Includes facts about mosquitoes.
  ISBN 978-1-58980-883-6 (hardcover : alk. paper) [1. Stories in
rhyme. 2. Mosquitoes—Fiction. 3. Animals—Fiction. 4. Humorous
stories.] I. LePlatt, Betsy, ill. II. Title.
  PZ8.3.K8997Mns 2011
  [E]—dc22
                                    2011005187

Printed in Singapore
Published by Pelican Publishing Company, Inc.
1000 Burmaster Street, Gretna, Louisiana 70053

MOSQUITO

**"Buzz," said Mosquito.
"Vamoose!" bellowed Moose.**

"Buzz," said Mosquito.
"Goodness gracious!"
honked Goose.

"Buzz," said Mosquito.
"Gee whiz!" growled Bear.

"Buzz," said Mosquito.
"Dagnabbit!" thumped Hare.

"Buzz," said Mosquito.
"How vicious!" said Vole.

"Buzz," said Mosquito.
"Holy moly!" squeaked Mole.

"Buzz," said Mosquito.
"Aw, shucks!" oinked Hog.

"Buzz," said Mosquito.
"Fiddlesticks!" barked Dog.

"Buzz," said Mosquito.
"Bah, bah!" bawled Lamb.

"Buzz," said Mosquito.
"Now scram!" bleated Ram.

"Buzz," said Mosquito.
"Boo, hiss," spewed Snake.

"Buzz," said Mosquito.
"Alack!" quacked Drake.

"Buzz," said Mosquito.
"Oh, bummer!" brayed
Burro.

"Buzz," said Mosquito.
"Skedaddle!" chirped
Sparrow.

"Buzz," said Mosquito.
"Dear me!" sighed Doe.

"Buzz," said Mosquito.
"Thunderation!" cawed Crow.

"Buzz," said Mosquito.
"Oh, nuts!" screeched Squirrel.

"Buzz," said Mosquito.
"Good heavens!" screamed Girl.

"Buzz," said Mosquito.
"Ah, drat!" snapped Rat.

"Buzz," said Mosquito.
"Oh, rats!" yowled Cat.

"Buzz," said Mosquito. . . .

"Gulp, *gulp!*" went Bat.

And that was that!

Mosquito Facts

A mosquito, whose name comes from the Spanish for "little fly," starts out as an egg laid in water in a raftlike structure with about one hundred other eggs. It hatches into a wriggly *larva,* then changes into a *pupa* (developing insect). When it flies off as an *adult,* it has already shed its skin several times.

Mosquitoes live in still water, from swamps to ponds, pitcher plants, puddles, and even rain-filled trashcan lids. They are pests not only because of their itchy stings but because those stings can pass along several serious diseases to humans and animals.

But a mosquito doesn't bite because she's mean. That's right, *she.* Only females buzz, and only females bite. Like male mosquitoes, they drink juices from flowers and plants. But when it comes time for her eggs to develop, a female needs protein and iron to nourish them, and she knows just where to find them.

She smells a *host* animal and lands lightly on its skin, which she pierces with her *proboscis,* a long, thin mouth tube. Besides sucking in blood like a straw, this tube delivers a chemical that keeps the host's blood flowing until the mosquito has her fill. If you spend time outdoors at night, it's a good idea to wear insect repellent so that you don't become a host.

Some fishes eat mosquito larvae, and birds and dragonflies catch adults on the wing. But many more mosquitoes are eaten by bats, the only mammals that truly fly.

By day, bats sleep upside down in trees, barns, deserted buildings, and caves and under eaves and cliffs. At dusk, they flutter out to feed on insects, which they catch while flying with their mouths open. A solitary bat can consume hundreds of insects in a single night, and flocks can keep some populations of mosquitoes under control.

Worldwide, there are about two thousand to three thousand species of mosquito.